D1375349

Illustra

Anneli Bray

For Leila of Ally Pally

First published in 2021 in Great Britain by
Barrington Stoke Ltd
18 Walker Street, Edinburgh, EH3 7LP

www.barringtonstoke.co.uk

A CIP catalogue record for this book is available
from the British Library upon request

ISBN: 978-1-78112-945-6

Printed by Hussar Books, Poland

Contents

CHAPTER 1

Ready, Steady, Jump!

I stood on the roof of the brick shed and looked up.

Above me I could see blue sky, dancing birds and puffy white clouds. Smoke drifted from the tall chimneys of nearby houses. How I wished I could swirl high into the sky like the smoke!

"Oi! Hurry up, Dolly!" my brother called out from the ground below.

David stared up at me. I was in my best dress and holding an umbrella upside down.

"I'll come when I'm ready, thank you!" I replied.

"Not scared, are you?" David asked with a cheeky grin.

"No chance!" I burst out.

I didn't mind David teasing me about being scared. He knew how brave I was. Don't get me wrong – my brother was brave too. He'd had awful nosebleeds his whole life and never ever moaned about them. But *I* was braver.

Not so long ago David got an answer wrong in class, and his teacher threw the blackboard cleaning block at his head. That one hard WHACK made David's nose bleed so badly his clothes got soaked with blood. The teacher shouted at David for making a mess. Well, that made me SO mad. The next day I marched into David's classroom to tell that teacher off. It didn't matter to me that I was skinny, small and younger than my brother. But the teacher ordered me out of the classroom before I got a chance to say a word! I was even madder then. I picked up an ink pot from the nearest desk – and threw it at the teacher. Let's see how HE liked his clothes all soaked and marked! The whole class cheered as that big bully of a teacher got what he deserved.

Mother and Father pretended to be cross with me, but I think they were proud that I'd tried to stand up for my brother. Even if it didn't end the way it was supposed to – I got expelled.

"Promise you won't tell Aunt Mariam when she comes to visit," Mother asked David and me.

Aunt Mariam was Mother's sister, and she was rich compared to us. She was a big, tall woman who wore huge hats and spotless gloves. She came to ours for afternoon tea once a month, on a Sunday. Father always told me and David to be on our best behaviour – as if we dared to be anything else! Of course Aunt

Mariam would still find fault with us, saying things like, "Sit up and don't slouch, Dolly!" and, "Use a hankie and don't sniff, David!" But even if she was bossy, Aunt Mariam was also kind. She always came with a box of fancy cakes and gave me and my brother warm hugs and pennies for pocket money when she left.

My mouth suddenly watered. Aunt Mariam was due here soon. What kind of cakes would she bring today? Lemon tarts or cherry slices? Or maybe cream horns! They were my favourite ...

"Come on, Dolly – jump!" David urged me now as I stood on the roof.

"I'm not going to jump," I called out to him. I picked up the black umbrella by the handle. "I'm going to fly!"

I saw the worried frown on my brother's face just as I was about to leap.

"Dolly Shepherd!" Aunt Mariam shouted at me, appearing round the corner in a wide purple hat. "What ARE you doing? Girls do NOT go clambering on roofs like that!"

"Why not?" I said. "*Boys* do."

I didn't mean to be cheeky. It was an honest question.

"I'm going to speak to your mother about this!" Aunt Mariam huffed and puffed. Her head was shaking so much it made the long feathers on her hat bob-bob-bob about.

"Mother won't mind," I told her.

Mother liked me being as brave and confident as any boy. She had trained me to ride our pony to and from the field every day since I was young – barefoot and without a saddle. Can you imagine if Aunt Mariam knew that?

"Get down this MINUTE, Dolly!" my aunt ordered.

"I was coming anyway," I said.

I held the umbrella above me, raised my chin up – and took a step into thin air ...

CHAPTER 2
Silly Ideas ...

"It's a wonder you didn't break your leg, Dolly!"
Aunt Mariam scolded me as she sat down at our
dining table.

"The shed wasn't high and I made sure
I jumped down onto a patch of grass. I was
perfectly safe," I said. My ankle ached a little,
but I didn't tell my aunt that!

"You let Dolly run wild!" Aunt Mariam
turned and complained to my parents.

I heard Father sigh as he stoked the fire. He knew there was no point arguing with Aunt Mariam. He might have been a policeman, but I think he was a bit scared of her!

I saw Mother move her apron to hide the mud on her skirt. She'd been helping break in a wild horse at the farm nearby this morning. Aunt Mariam would not approve of that either.

"Dolly just has a lot of spirit," Mother said as she poured tea into our best china cups. "Like you, Mariam dear."

"Well, I ... hmm," Aunt Mariam muttered.

She didn't seem to know what to say to that. Aunt Mariam might not have been the sort of person to jump off roofs, but she was fearless too. She was a woman running her own company. Aunt Mariam was scared of nothing and no one.

She took a sip of her tea, then turned to me and my brother. "So, tell me your news, children," Aunt Mariam said.

David and I went silent, thinking of all the things we loved and enjoyed that Aunt Mariam would not like.

"Well?" Aunt Mariam tried again.

Suddenly David spoke. And he was saying *exactly* the wrong thing.

"Dolly acted in a show yesterday!" he said. "She was very good!"

"*Acted?* In a *show?*" said Aunt Mariam. She made it sound as if I'd joined a gang of crooks and become a pickpocket.

"I saw an advert in the local newspaper," I explained. "They wanted young actors for a show at the theatre at Alexandra Palace."

Alexandra Palace was a grand building on top of a hill close to where we lived. It was the most amazing place – a "palace for the people" as everyone said, not for kings and queens! It even had a nickname: "Ally Pally". Every Saturday and Sunday ordinary people visited the Ally Pally funfair and showground to see marvels like acrobats and fireworks. There had even been an elephant paraded around the boating lake! Bands played, spectacular balloon rides happened ... and theatre shows too.

"Dolly played a dead girl in the show," David went on. "She was very good – till she sneezed and the whole audience burst out laughing!"

Aunt Mariam looked as if she would never laugh again. She just turned and stared hard at Mother.

Mother played with the handle of her teacup, looking uncomfortable. "We thought it wouldn't do any harm."

"Pardon me, but NO niece of mine is going to be an *actress*!" Aunt Mariam snapped. "Dolly needs to get these silly ideas out of her head. In fact, I think she should come to work for me when she turns sixteen in a few months. I can train her up."

The tall feathers on Aunt Mariam's hat bobbed about again. Feathers were her work – she ran the Ostrich Feather Emporium in the heart of London. Boxes of these feathers would arrive from Africa and Egypt, then be dyed different colours and sewn onto hats for rich women to buy.

Father, Mother and David looked at me, their eyes wide. They knew this was important. Aunt Mariam wanted to take me into her successful business. Maybe she expected me to replace her as the boss one day. I needed to thank Aunt Mariam.

But all I could do was stare at the bobbing feathers on her hat and say something stupid.

"Flying must be so wonderful," I said. "Do you think ostriches are sad that their wings don't work?"

Aunt Mariam rolled her eyes and sighed ...

CHAPTER 3
Snatching Chances

My life was about to change. I was sixteen years old, and on Monday morning I'd be working in the heart of London for my aunt. But today I was just going to have fun at Ally Pally! I got off the train and followed the Saturday crowds up the hill.

Everyone looked very smartly dressed. They were probably maids and shop workers and tradesmen on their days off, all in their best clothes.

"I can't wait to see Mr Sousa, Father!" I heard a young girl in front of me say.

I smiled. I was excited about Mr Sousa myself. He was a very famous band leader, all the way from America, and *everyone* knew his tunes! I'd come here today to see him perform. But I had one problem ... I didn't have a ticket. Mother and Father made sure David and I had plenty to eat and good clothes to wear, but we did not have any money for treats like seeing Mr Sousa.

Still, I had a plan ... I moved away from the crowds and hurried up a path that took me to the back of Ally Pally. I knew a door there led to the kitchens of the building.

I took a deep breath and knocked on it. A frowning woman yanked the door open.

"Yes?" she grunted.

"Do you need extra staff today?" I said as confidently as I could manage.

The woman looked me up and down. I was glad I'd worn my long black wool dress. I knew it made me look the part.

"You're a waitress?" she asked.

"Yes," I lied. The only people I'd ever "served" were Mother, Father and David. And Aunt Mariam too, of course.

"Very well," said the woman. "Follow me!"

I hurried after her, first through the busy kitchens and then upstairs into a huge hall with lovely stained-glass windows. At one end was a cafe. At the other end was the stage where the great Mr Sousa would be performing this afternoon.

"Here," said the woman, handing me an apron. "Make yourself busy."

As she walked away, I bit my lip. I had no idea what to do! But I watched the other waitresses like a hawk and soon got the hang of things.

The time grew closer for the concert to start and I was smiling, unlike the two customers who had just sat down at a table nearby. As I waited to take their order, I saw that the two men looked worried. One of the men wore a navy-blue uniform, while the other was dressed as a Wild West cowboy with long hair and a scruffy beard. Wait – was this the showman Colonel Samuel Cody? I wondered. I had seen his image on posters for Ally Pally! He did lots of daring acts, such as making his horse prance on its hind legs and shooting at a target – which happened to be an egg sitting on his wife's head …

I was about to ask what the men would like to order when I heard the man in the navy uniform speak.

"This is dreadful," he said in a soft French accent. "Everyone loves your shooting act, Colonel Cody. If Mrs Cody cannot do the show later, you'll have to cancel."

I stood there with my notepad in my hand. My happiness at being in Ally Pally made me braver than brave.

Out came the words, "Don't cancel it, sir. *I* can help. I can be in your show!"

The two men turned to me.

"Really? You would do that?" asked the cowboy.

"Why not?" I replied.

I tried not to think of Aunt Mariam and how many reasons she'd have for me not to do it!

CHAPTER 4
Ready or Not?

What a day! So far I had seen the wonderful Mr Sousa and his band play – for free. I had earned good money for waitressing before and afterwards. And now I was standing at the side of the stage of the theatre at Ally Pally, about to star in Colonel Cody's shooting act!

I peeked out from behind the red velvet curtains to look at the audience. What would they think of an ordinary young girl like me stepping in for Mrs Cody?

Then I sensed someone standing beside me. It was the man who'd been with Colonel Cody earlier. This close up, I saw that he had a hot-air balloon stitched on the collar of his uniform. I realised who he was ... I'd also seen him on posters for Ally Pally. This man was Captain Gaudron, who piloted hot-air balloons – and sometimes jumped out of them, to gasps from the crowds below!

"Are you ready, Miss Shepherd?" Captain Gaudron asked me. "Not too nervous, I hope?"

"Not at all – I'm excited!" I told him.

"Good," said Captain Gaudron with a steady nod. "Colonel Cody is a fine marksman."

Captain Gaudron had a serious but kind face and a calm voice. His words and his manner made me even more certain that this was a wonderful opportunity for a girl like me. A chance to be in the spotlight!

"Will you all welcome Miss Dolly Shepherd," Colonel Cody called out. "She has kindly agreed to help me this evening."

I almost skipped up onto the stage to the sounds of cheers and applause. There were surprised murmurs too when people saw how young I was. Colonel Cody waved me over to join him. He had a smile a mile wide and was holding a shotgun! He then ushered me to stand at a particular spot on the stage and took an egg from his pocket. He placed it carefully on top of my head.

"Stay quite still!" Colonel Cody told me.

"Of course," I whispered. I didn't move a muscle, not even my lips!

I wasn't worried – until I saw Captain Gaudron take a silk scarf from his pocket and tie it over Colonel Cody's eyes. Oh dear ... I didn't know he was going to be blindfolded! But before I had a second to worry, the shot

had been fired – and bits of egg splattered
everywhere.

The watching crowd gasped and clapped. But I burst out laughing!

How thrilling was that?

Captain Gaudron led me back to the side of the stage, and I turned to smile at the audience. I spotted that a woman in the front row had fainted! A box of chocolates had slid off her lap, and the sweets were scattered at her feet.

My, my ... what a stir little Dolly Shepherd had caused!

CHAPTER 5

A Step into Another World

I was presented with a box of chocolates of my own from Colonel Cody. But the real reward for my help in his shooting act came the next morning. Captain Gaudron had offered to give me a tour of the huge workshop in the grounds of Ally Pally where the hot-air balloons were kept.

To see these marvels up close would be such a treat! David came with me, but he had different ideas ...

"It's just a sort of warehouse," David muttered as we stood in the doorway staring in. He didn't seem that interested in the sight of the huge coloured balloons hanging limp from the ceiling, the giant baskets and the equipment stored next to them.

"You want to go and meet your friends at the fairground, don't you?" I asked him.

David glanced around and saw that I would be safe here. There were several women working away on rattling sewing machines. The double doors were open wide and members of the public strolled by. And here came Captain Gaudron, who gave us a welcoming hello.

"Well, yes," said David. "I'd like to see my friends. I'll come back for you in an hour, Dolly. Take care."

"I'll be fine," I told David firmly, and took a step into the workshop. A step into another world ...

First, Captain Gaudron introduced me to the women who were sewing silk parachutes. Next he explained how the balloons worked. Some were filled with hot air from fires and others were piped full of gas. The balloons would then gently whoosh into the sky with a basket of excited passengers hanging below. Captain Gaudron told me how he sometimes let another pilot take over, while he leapt from the basket with his parachute and floated to the ground, unharmed!

"But how?" I asked with a puzzled frown. "How is the parachute attached to you? And how does it open?"

"Let me demonstrate," said Captain Gaudron. He walked over to a soft silk shape hanging from a hook on the wall. "Imagine this parachute as a closed umbrella. And the very tip of it is attached to the netting of the balloon by a cord."

I nodded. I could picture it so far.

"Now see this?" Captain Gaudron said. He pointed to two thick ropes and a wooden trapeze bar that dangled below the slumped parachute. "Imagine this as the 'handle' of the umbrella. I jump from the basket of the hot-air balloon and hold on tight to the bar with both hands. My weight snaps the cord like *that*!"

Captain Gaudron clicked his fingers.

"It's very simple," he went on. "As I fall, the design of the parachute makes it puff open."

He had explained it well, I thought, but it sounded far from simple!

"Don't your arms ache?" I asked.

"Yes, but look – there's a canvas sling that hangs from the trapeze bar. I rest one leg over it, and it helps take some of my weight."

I peered at the sling. The loop of material reminded me of a bandage.

"Here – put your leg through it," said
Captain Gaudron. "And reach up to the bar as
I hold it."

"Hey, Dolly!" I heard my name called.

It was David. Could an hour truly have passed already? And how silly must I have looked with my arms in the air clutching a wooden bar, my leg hooked over a sling and my long skirt crumpled!

"We'd better get going – if you're not in too much of a tangle," David teased me. "Remember, Mother said you need to pack for tomorrow."

Yes, of course. I had to pack for my new life with Aunt Mariam. And I needed to leave Captain Gaudron and his balloons behind.

Or so I thought ...

CHAPTER 6

Promises, Promises ...

It was the end of my first week working for Aunt Mariam.

The other girls at the Ostrich Feather Emporium had not been very friendly at first. I understood why – I was the boss's niece. Maybe they expected Aunt Mariam to give me an easy time of it. But she expected me to learn ALL the jobs that needed doing ...

"I didn't know how smelly feathers were," I said to a kind-looking girl called Louie-May.

"And how hard it is to make them pretty enough for a hat!"

Louie-May had shown me how to clean grease off the dirty brown feathers. Then how to bleach them white. Then how to dip the feathers in the vats of different coloured dye. (All the bleaching and dyeing chemicals nipped the inside of my nose and burned the skin on my fingers!)

I was holding a newly dyed pink feather above my head and parading about like I was a fancy lady. Louie-May and the other girls roared and laughed. Then they stopped – and I guessed who had just walked in.

"Oh. Hello, Aunt Mariam ..." I said, letting the pink feather drop to my side.

"Hmmff," my aunt muttered. "Here – your mother has sent you a note. I don't know what the hurry is. You'll be home with her tomorrow."

My tummy flipped as I took the note. The plan was for me to stay with Aunt Mariam during the week to be close to work, and to go back home from Friday evening till Monday morning. So my aunt was right – why did Mother want to contact me in a hurry? The note had to be important.

Dolly – this came for you.
Love, Mother

Inside Mother's note was a slim envelope. I tore it open.

Dear Miss Shepherd,

I got your address from the cafe at Alexandra Palace. I hope you don't mind me writing, but I wondered if you might be interested in joining my aerial display team ...

My eyes sped to read the rest of the letter. It was from Captain Gaudron. If I was keen, I had to meet him at Ally Pally the next day.

"What is this?" asked Aunt Mariam. "Is it from an admirer?" She snatched the letter from my hand. How funny – she suspected it was a love letter from a boy!

"No, it's nothing like that," I tried to explain. "Captain Gaudron is a well-respected gentleman."

"But what does he mean by this?" Aunt Mariam asked. "What is an 'aerial display team'?"

"Oh, Aunt Mariam!" I said. "Captain Gaudron wants me to be an aeronaut!" I should not have answered like this. But I was so thrilled, the words spilled out.

"A what-a-not?" my aunt asked.

"An aer-o-naut." I said the tricky word more clearly. I was about to explain that it meant someone who flies in the air, but Aunt Mariam spoke first.

"You mean one of those fools who go up in balloons?" she said.

Yes, it could mean that. But I suspected Captain Gaudron did not want me IN the big

basket of his hot-air balloon. That was for pilots and paying customers. He wanted me to do what he sometimes did.

"No," I said. "I think he wants me to jump from the balloon. With a parachute, of course!"

"What?" Aunt Mariam gasped, putting her hand to her chest. "Who is this dreadful man? Asking my darling niece to fall from the sky? To risk her life for a silly fairground stunt? You are NOT to do this, Dolly. Promise me!"

I looked at my horrified aunt. I looked at the faces of all the girls in the workroom.

I folded up the letter and put it in my pocket.

"Good girl," said Aunt Mariam with a sigh of relief.

She thought that was the end of it.

But I had NOT made any promises ...

CHAPTER 7

Up, Up and Away!

It was busy on the grassy slopes of Ally Pally the next day. The swarming crowd below gave a great cheer as a huge golden balloon rose slowly into the sky.

The wicker basket underneath the balloon swayed and creaked like an old sailing ship. I was sitting on the very edge of it – perched like a pigeon on a chimney pot!

Inside the basket, Captain Gaudron held tight to the thick cords that helped him steer and control the balloon. The three paying

passengers gasped as the park, palace and trees
began to shrink below as we rose higher.

How I wished Mother, Father and David were in the crowd beneath my feet. But when I'd told them about Captain Gaudron's invitation they said they didn't have the nerve to come and watch. I understood – and I knew they were proud of me.

"I can't believe a young girl like you can do something so daring!" said one of the two male passengers.

"But why not?" I said cheerfully. Truthfully, I was finding it hard to talk. The view was so amazing. The sensation of lifting up, UP, UP was astounding.

With one hand I held tight to a stiff rope that linked the basket to the balloon. My other hand held on to the wooden trapeze bar attached to the floppy parachute above my head. I glanced at my bunched skirt – I'd pinned it between my legs so I didn't show off my long underwear on the way down!

I hoped the pins would stay in place. I hoped the canvas sling under my thigh would support me. I hoped my white knuckles would hold tight to the wooden bar as I fell ...

"How many times have you done this, Miss Shepherd?" the female passenger asked me.

"I can't count," I replied.

That was true. I couldn't count because I had never done it before! And this would be my one and only trip into the sky. I'd decided I'd have this wonderful experience and never do it again. Aunt Mariam would never know I had been here. All the way up in the air, floating side by side with the birds!

"Do you think anyone will ever truly fly?" the other male passenger asked Captain Gaudron. "In a machine, I mean?"

"Of course!" said the captain. "There are many men working on it now, in America and Europe. It might happen very soon."

Men, I thought, swinging my feet in the air. *Why just men? Why can't women dream and build and succeed too?* It didn't seem fair ...

"Will flying machines happen in my lifetime?" the passenger went on.

"Yes, soon! I expect it to happen in the next few years," said Captain Gaudron. "But for now it is people such as myself and Miss Dolly Shepherd who own the sky. Isn't that right, Dolly?"

"Yes," I said in a very confident voice.

Ha! What would the passengers think if they knew I'd only had half an hour's training before we took to the air today?

"And actually, I think it is nearly time, Dolly," the captain said. "With the wind in this direction, aim for that field over there."

I looked where he pointed and nodded. I had to trust him. I had no other choice at this stage.

"Ready?" Captain Gaudron said.

"Ready!" I replied.

And then came the order.

"HANDS OFF!" Captain Gaudron shouted clearly.

I let go of the basket rope.

"Cheerio!" I called to the passengers as their mouths gaped open.

Both my hands were now on the trapeze bar. I was tumbling off the side of the basket, grateful for the canvas sling that held some of my weight.

But then I dropped. I dropped like a stone.

I couldn't breathe with the sheer shock of it all.

It felt as if my body was made of bricks as I sped down towards the ground.

Was this it?

Was I going to die today?

Would I never see David's and my parents' dear faces again?

Should I have listened to the warnings and worries of my aunt?

And then WHOOOOSH!

It happened. Just as Captain Gaudron said it would. The floppy parachute gulped great pockets of air and filled into a vast silk dome above my head. Instead of plummeting, I was now swaying, free and easy.

I laughed.

I laughed into the silent sky as I wiggled my feet around, walking on air – no, dancing. I was dancing on air!

But then I realised I must be sensible. Time was running out already. I had to land, and there was the field Captain Gaudron had pointed out. I tugged the cords in the right direction and watched, surprised, as the green grassy ground sped right up towards me.

BOOF!

My feet touched down. I bent my knees and tossed myself backwards into a roll, as quick as a wink. Captain Gaudron had said that this would spread the shock across my body and help prevent any broken bones. I lay there panting on the grass with my eyes closed, letting my shaking body feel the safety of the firm earth.

But my quiet moment didn't last long. I was not alone. Something in that field had watched me fall and now wanted to know that I was all right.

The long, rasping tongue of a cow nearly ripped the skin off my cheek!

"Oi!" I called to the cow. "Leave me alone!"

Then the man who had been sent on a horse and cart to collect me and bring me back to Ally Pally arrived. What must I have looked like to him?

A silly girl shooing a curious cow away after having just fallen to the ground?

Or a guilty girl who knew she couldn't keep her promise to herself?

So much for only jumping once – I HAD to do that again!

CHAPTER 8
Saved by a Smash

I jumped at Ally Pally every weekend for many weeks and loved every thrilling second of it.

Mother, Father and David still hadn't worked up the courage to come and see me in action yet, but they eagerly pestered me for every last detail!

Aunt Mariam knew nothing of my adventures. But my workmates did. Every Monday morning I'd tell the girls about my latest jumps as we sat scraping the grease off ostrich feathers. Today I was telling them about something new – a solo flight.

"I don't understand," said Louie-May with a frown. "What is a solo flight?"

"I'm not jumping from the basket of a hot-air balloon any more," I explained. "I now have my *own* balloon. There's no basket, no pilot and no passengers. The balloon is filled with gas and then lifts me up on my trapeze bar ..."

"Just you and a balloon, floating all by yourselves?" asked Louie-May with a dreamy look in her eyes. "How magical that must be!"

"It is," I agreed.

"Well, I don't believe you," said a grumpy girl called Bessie. "How can you be all alone up there? How do you get back down without help?"

I wiped my hand clean on my apron and pulled something out of my pocket. It was small and round like a watch face.

"This is called an aneroid," I told Bessie, Louie-May and the others. "It gets tied around my wrist. It shows me the air pressure and how high I am. Once I am up to two thousand feet,

I get ready to drop. The release happens in a different way, since there's no basket to jump off. I tug a cord that pulls a pin, and that frees my parachute from the balloon. Then I start falling and—"

"Dolly ... my office, NOW," Aunt Mariam said sharply from the doorway. She must have heard everything.

I followed her silently. She whacked the door shut and stood by the fire burning in the grate. Aunt Mariam looked furious and worried. Finally she talked.

"Did I not forbid you to do parachute stunts?"

My aunt's voice was stern, but I saw her bottom lip was trembling. She cared about me very much.

"Yes, Aunt Mariam," I replied. "But it really is the most wonderful feeling in the world to—"

"Do your parents know?" Aunt Mariam demanded.

"Yes," I said. "They think it's fine as long as I promise to stay safe."

Aunt Mariam let out a long, tired sigh and shook her head.

"Dolly," she said at last, "I cannot bear to think of you doing something so dangerous. I cannot bear to imagine losing you."

"But I really am always safe!" I tried to insist. "Captain Gaudron checks all the equipment before I—"

Aunt Mariam held her hand up to stop me.

"If you choose to carry on with these stunts, Dolly, I need you to promise me one thing. You will NEVER tell me about them."

"Oh, Aunt Mariam, I—"

The promise never left my lips. A loud SMASH cut me off.

"What was that?" I asked, shocked at the sound. "Did someone just break the shop window?"

"Some suffragettes have been causing trouble around here the last few days," said Aunt Mariam as she hurried out of her office. "They've broken lots of shop windows nearby!"

I didn't ask why. I knew already – the suffragettes wanted women to have the same rights as men, to be able to vote as men did. They protested in many ways, and one was to break the windows of shops that sold luxury goods, like the Ostrich Feather Emporium. The suffragettes thought women should be more interested in politics than fashion.

I went to follow Aunt Mariam but spotted a newspaper on her desk. It was neatly folded – she hadn't read it yet. But there was a story on the front page ... about the death of a parachutist at a fair in the north of England!

With a gulp, I picked up that paper and tore it to shreds. I threw the shreds into the roaring fire and then left the room.

Aunt Mariam didn't need to see that story and worry. Yes, I felt so very sorry for the girl who'd had the accident, but it wasn't going to stop me from jumping. I was doing something that so few people in the world had ever done. And hardly any females! It might have been for fairground entertainment, but I was an aeronaut. A *girl* aeronaut. I had a feeling the suffragettes would be proud of me!

And as I said to Aunt Mariam, I was always safe. I'd never had the slightest problem with a jump. So what was there to worry about?

CHAPTER 9

Stuck in the Sky

Captain Gaudron's aerial display team soon went on to appear in showgrounds in other towns and cities – me included. It was so exciting to travel there and back on steam trains.

My parents had come to know Captain Gaudron well and trusted that he would take good care of me. They asked just one thing on the days when I was far from home. I had to send them a telegram to say I was safe just as soon as my jump was done.

One breezy day I was in a town that was new to me. I felt relaxed, as I'd already found out where the nearest telegraph office was and arranged for someone to go there for me later. I strolled around the waiting crowd, saying hello, shaking hands, being treated like royalty.

"Hello, miss!" a cheeky-faced boy called out. "Why are you wearing such funny trousers?"

"Shush!" his shocked mother said.

"It's fine," I said with a smile. "This is my aeronaut uniform."

I wasn't surprised the boy was curious. There were lots of girls and women at the showground, but none dressed like me. Captain Gaudron had arranged for me to have a special outfit, like the other team members – a navy-blue suit and hat with gold buttons and trim. But instead of a skirt I wore a type of baggy trousers that gathered tight below my knees. They were SO comfortable compared to

a heavy long skirt. But they were SO shocking for a girl to wear, because they *weren't* a skirt!

"These trousers are called knickerbockers," I explained to the boy.

"Knickerbockers!" the boy said, and laughed at the silly-sounding name. "Do they help you fly?"

"Yes indeed!" I told him. "But I'd better go ... it's nearly time for my jump."

I gave him a wave as I walked away to join Captain Gaudron and do the final safety checks.

"Miss!" I heard the boy call out. "Don't get lost in all them clouds up there, will you!"

"I won't!" I called back, but my words were drowned out by the hiss of the gas filling the balloon.

Minutes later I was high in the silent sky, swaying from the trapeze bar below my solo balloon. Back on the ground the watching crowds turned into pinpricks, the buildings to dolls' houses, and nearby fields to pieces of green patchwork. What a joy this was – to sail on the breeze, to see a view from above that most people could only dream of. Here I was, just an ordinary girl in this wonderland between the earth and the sky. How lucky was I?

I looked up at my wrist. The aneroid said two thousand feet. Perfect! Time for me and my parachute to say cheerio to the balloon and drift back down.

I tugged the release cord.

Nothing happened.

I tugged it again.

And again.

And again and again and again ... But nothing. The pin was jammed!

"Well, then," I said to the balloon above me. "I'll just have to wait till you start to lose gas and drift down yourself."

Shocked as I was, I knew that was exactly what would happen. At every show a horse and cart was sent for me as I landed. Another horse and cart followed the balloon till it finally ran out of gas. But that could take hours and land miles away ... Could I last that long? Wouldn't my arms get too tired, even with the sling taking some of my weight?

I gave myself a shake. It was pointless to think like this. Getting scared wouldn't do any good. I had to be strong.

"Come on, Dolly!" I said to myself. "You'll just have to manage. How about a song?"

I sang a cheerful tune my father liked. The far-away ground looked so blurred now and the roads were as thin as thread.

I sang a pretty hymn my mother loved. The air grew colder the higher I got, and my arms began to ache badly.

I sang a funny song my brother adored. Everything became misty as I entered a haze of cotton wool. I was lost in the clouds ... just what the cheeky-faced little boy from earlier told me not to do!

And then with a puff I suddenly found myself in the most incredible place. *Above* the clouds. Just me and my balloon in a vast empty sky with a white carpet of cloud below. No ground, no earth to be seen. I couldn't describe this. Captain Gaudron had never told me I could find myself so extremely high! It was beyond stunning – and beyond terrifying. I had never felt so amazed – and never felt so alone.

I wanted to look at this beautiful sight for ever. At the same time I would have given anything to be far away from it with my feet back on solid ground.

I glanced at my aneroid and saw I was now about two miles above the earth. Panic started

to bite at me as much as the cold. And so I did
the only thing I could – I kept singing!

Song after song after song. Shouting the
words into the empty air.

Shouting till I was so crazy that I thought I heard a brass band playing.

Only it WAS a brass band!

I was now gently drifting back down, thanks to my balloon *finally* losing gas. There was the showground, far in the distance. The wind was whipping the sound of the band my way as if to let me know all was well!

And then I was tumbling, rolling to safety on the ground. I realised I was in the middle of a field with a farmer staring at me, completely shocked!

"Quick! I need to get to the showground!" I babbled.

Bless the farmer, who jumped into action, hurrying to get his bike from the barn. In no time at all I was perched on the back, racing and bumping down lanes as the kind farmer pedalled like mad.

He parked right by the bandstand, and I raced up and grabbed the baton from the conductor.

I stood there grinning in front of the crowd as the loudest roar and cheer went up. I hoped the cheeky-faced little boy was among them and hadn't been too scared for me. And I saw Captain Gaudron running towards the bandstand, a big relieved smile on his normally serious face.

"Dolly! We thought we'd lost you!" I heard Captain Gaudron call out.

"Oh, I wasn't lost!" I called back. "Just off on an adventure!"

The whole crowd burst out laughing at that. I just hoped no one could see how much my legs were shaking inside my "funny" baggy trousers ...

CHAPTER 10

Red Mist

The adventures kept coming for me. I did jump after jump, week after week, showground after showground. Father finally agreed to come along to a few, but Mother and David were still working up the courage. *One day*, I thought, *one day.*

In the meantime, I kept my promise to Aunt Mariam. She never heard a thing about my jumps. The girls at the Ostrich Feather Emporium made sure the door of the workroom was firmly shut when they begged me to tell them what I'd been up to!

I'd done dozens of parachute jumps by now. Some days the sun beat down on me, sometimes the wind whirled me in circles. But every time I jumped I marvelled at the chance I had been given. I would never give it up. Never. Even if once in a while things went a bit wrong ...

"You were clinging to a chimney?" said Louie-May, her blue eyes wide.

"Clinging on for dear life!" I told her and the others over our cups of tea. "I got blown onto the factory roof and could have slid right off. I was so grateful for that chimney!"

"But how did you get down?" the new girl, Ada, asked me.

"I was hanging on to the chimney when this face popped up at the edge of the roof," I said. "A man on a tall ladder. He told me to let go so I would slip down towards him and he would catch me. It was only a little way, but I was *so* scared. I yelled to him, 'I'd rather drop two miles out of the sky than do that!'"

All the girls burst out laughing at my story. Everyone but Bessie. She sat perched on the edge of a large vat of dye, staring at me.

"Tell Ada about the time with the train!" Louie-May begged me.

"Yes, yes, yes!" the others cheered me on – all but Bessie.

"Well, I was coming down towards a field when the wind whipped me away," I began. "I was dipping low and spinning every which way. Then my cords spun me around – and I saw a train hurtling towards me, bellowing steam! My toes were nearly tapping on the roof of the first train carriage, but then another gust of wind lifted me up and into a field."

"So you were safe?" Ada asked with a sigh of relief.

"She was – sort of!" Louie-May sniggered. "Tell her what happened next, Dolly!"

"Well, I got blown into the fence of the field. A *barbed-wire* fence!"

Shocked, Ada's hand went to her mouth as the other girls giggled. They already knew the end of this story!

"I wasn't really hurt," I said. "Just pricked and scratched. But I was totally stuck! The barbs dug into my clothes, and I couldn't get free. Luckily, a young man had been walking nearby and ran to help. *Unluckily*, the barbs had torn my knickerbockers right off me. I was hanging there in my underwear!"

The whole workroom exploded with laughter. It didn't matter how many times I'd told that embarrassing story, the girls always ended up howling and crying with delight. All except Bessie.

"I don't believe you," Bessie said, staring daggers at me. "Not a word, Dolly Shepherd."

It had been a long time since I'd felt so angry. Not since I'd foolishly thrown ink over my brother's teacher. But I'd had enough of Bessie. I used the money I made from jumping to buy sweets and cakes and treats for everyone every Monday morning. I didn't tell the girls my stories to show off. I told them to share something amazing. I hoped that, like me, *they* would all get the chance to do amazing things sometime in their lives.

But a red mist of rage had come over me. I hurried over to the glaring Bessie and pushed her sharp and hard. She fell right back into the vat of purple dye with a screech!

That serves her right, I thought angrily to myself.

But the very next moment I was sorry I had done it.

Those magical times of floating free in the sky had taught me that silly worries and petty arguments didn't matter at all. Not at all!

Yet here I was getting stupidly cross with Bessie. Maybe her life was very hard. Maybe no one else in her family was making any money, and her wages had to feed her brothers and sisters.

As I hurried to help Bessie out of the vat of dye I decided something. From now on I would *always* be my best self. Someone my parents and my brother, my darling aunt and Captain Gaudron could be proud of.

Yes, I might have been a girl with her head in the clouds, but I'd aim to have kindness in my heart at all times. At least, I'd try!

CHAPTER 11
Alone Together

My friend Louie-May had been coming to see me jump every time we were at Ally Pally. Louie-May was bright, bubbly and strong. I had introduced her to Captain Gaudron after one of my jumps ... and Louie-May asked if she could jump one day too!

Now that day had come.

The showground at Ally Pally was heaving with people, and they all seemed to be gathered around our balloon, waiting for the display to start.

"Are you all right?" I asked Louie-May.

It was to be a smaller solo balloon flight –
but with TWO women on it. A "double descent",
Captain Gaudron called it! Louie-May and I were
attached to either side of the whooshing, filling
balloon, far enough away from each other so
that our floppy parachutes and trapeze ropes
wouldn't get tangled together on the way up.

"Yes, I'm all right," Louie-May replied to
my question. But I saw her chest heave as she
breathed fast in and out.

"Remember what I told you," I said.

I didn't just mean the safety instructions. I
meant the stunning things we would see from
up there.

"I wouldn't miss this for the world!"
Louie-May said cheerfully.

And then the balloon lifted, and we were off.

In those first few seconds I watched
Louie-May as she gasped, shocked at our sudden
silent rise away from the ground. And then I
saw her look down and smile.

"How is this possible?" she said with a laugh. "I can't believe I am here! It is as wonderful as you said, Dolly!"

"Isn't it?" I said, dancing my feet in the air.

"I forgot to ask – how long are we up here for?" said Louie-May.

"Only a few minutes up and a few minutes down," I told her. "So enjoy the view while you can – in fact, we are nearly ready to drop."

"Already?" said Louie-May, dangling from her trapeze bar. "It's so soon! I wish we could stay up here a bit longer ..."

I looked up at my wrist. The aneroid was at two thousand feet. It was time to go.

"Pull your cord now. I'll be right behind you!" I called out, ready to watch Louie-May fall – until her parachute filled with air and she would glide down, with me close behind. What fun!

Except ...

Except I watched Louie-May pull at her cord ... and nothing happened. She stared at me, wondering what was happening.

She pulled again. And again.

No! This had happened to me before, of course. But poor Louie-May! This was her first ever jump. And here she was, stuck in the sky as I had been.

"What is it?" my friend shouted over to me. "What's wrong? Don't I drop now?"

"Try again!" I shouted back as we rose higher and higher, my aneroid ticking away as we soared.

"It's not working!" said Louie-May. "What do I do?"

"You do nothing," I told my friend as I swayed on my bar. "This happened to me once, remember? We have to hang on till the gas escapes from the balloon."

"What? For how long? Oh ... what is this? What is happening, Dolly?"

We were soaring up and into the clouds, hidden from each other as if we were in fog. And then we came out the other side – we were above the clouds now.

Louie-May let out an awful scream.

"Where is the ground? Where IS everything, Dolly?!" she screeched.

"Don't panic," I told her, forcing my voice to be sure and strong. "Don't look up or down, Louie-May. Look at my face."

My friend did as I ordered and looked straight at me. Her eyes were full of fear and her cheeks were streaked with tears. This was bad. Poor Louie-May was clearly petrified. Shock was making her tremble, and I didn't know how long she'd manage to hold on to her trapeze bar, even with the sling under her leg. And then I realised that her lips were turning blue with the cold, and I knew I had to act fast. Any minute now she might lose her grip and fall ...

"Listen to me, Louie-May," I called out. "When I say go, we are going to start swinging towards each other. When we are close enough, I will grab you. We are going to go down together on my parachute. Do you understand?"

Louie-May nodded hard, her teeth chattering. Of course I was worried. This had never been done before. Could my trusty little parachute hold the two of us? Or would it crumple and let us drop like rocks onto the earth below? Those questions flashed into my mind, but what choice did we have?

"One, two, three ... swing towards me!" I said.

It took several swings, but then she was close. I quickly reached out with one arm and yanked Louie-May to me.

"Wrap your legs around my waist!" I ordered my terrified friend. I felt Louie-May do it. "Now transfer your hands to MY trapeze bar, one at a time ..."

THUNK!

One hand.

THUNK!

The other.

She'd done it. Louie-May's trapeze bar swung loose and spun behind her. We were face to face.

"Well done!" I told her with as bright a smile as I could manage. "You're so brave."

"No, I'm not!" Louie-May said, panicked. "I can't do this – my fingers are so cold I can barely feel them. I can't hold on, Dolly!"

My mind raced and luckily came up with a solution.

"Let go of my trapeze bar one hand at a time," I told her. "Wrap one arm and then the other around me – as if you are a child hugging their mother. Do it NOW!"

My order left Louie-May no time to think, and with a heavy jolt I felt the whole weight of her body on mine. I had to act fast, as I wasn't sure how long I could hold us both …

I tugged the release cord of my parachute sharply.

SNAP went the sound.

And we dropped, dropped, dropped down into the clouds at top speed. Louie-May clung tight to me for dear life, her screams in my ears.

And then WHOOSH!

My trusty parachute gulped at the air and opened in a wide, comforting arc above us.

Below was the tangle of green fields and grey buildings and bustle of life as we knew it.

The carpet of earth rushed to meet us at eye-watering speed.

"Remember to roll!" I called out as we came hurtling down.

But there was no chance for either of us to roll, not locked together as we were.

The soft mud of the field embraced us. I heard Louie-May sob as she got to her feet, crying with happiness that she wasn't dead or injured.

As for me, I lay still and silent. I couldn't get up. Something was very, very wrong …

CHAPTER 12

Hopeful Dreams?

The view from my bed was wonderful. It was as if I was lying in a florist's shop! Vases and jugs filled with bunches of flowers were on every surface. And dotted between them were countless cards and telegrams wishing me a speedy recovery. I had no idea so many people cared about me!

But I wasn't in my *own* bed. My back injury from the fall was too bad for me to be moved far. The farmer whose field Louie-May and I had landed in took me to his cottage, using an unscrewed door as a stretcher. He and his wife and children couldn't have been better or more caring nurses. I just wished I could remember the first few days ... but I'd kept slipping into a deep dark sleep of pain. I didn't even remember Captain Gaudron visiting me, or Father. But I was a bit better now – though I still couldn't feel my legs. I was able to chat cheerfully to the person who sat in the chair beside my bed.

"The two girls who found themselves in difficulty in mid-air both behaved with remarkable grit and heroism," Aunt Mariam read from the newspaper.

"I can't say we were heroes," I said with a small smile. "We just did what we had to do to get ourselves back on the ground safely. And all that matters to me is that Louie-May was not badly hurt."

"Oh, you're so brave, Dolly!" Aunt Mariam said with tears in her eyes. "I can't believe you'll never walk again."

"What?" I said, trying to push myself up on the pillows and wincing. "No, no, Aunt Mariam! The *first* doctor thought that. But I have seen another yesterday, and he is sure I will be well again soon."

Aunt Mariam reached over and patted my arm with her gloved hand. I guessed she wondered if I was holding on to some hopeful dream rather than facing the awful truth.

"Honestly, I believe him!" I tried to explain. "Dr Allan tried out a new invention on me. He attached these metal plates to my back and legs, then sent electric currents into them. I felt these jags all over. He said he will do it again and again, and it will shock the muscles and nerves that are paralysed."

"*Electric currents!*" Aunt Mariam gasped, horrified, clutching at her chest. She clearly disapproved of Dr Allan and his treatment as much as she did of Captain Gaudron and his airborne adventures.

I wasn't sure I'd be able to convince my aunt about this very modern treatment. But with a little time and effort I would show Aunt Mariam it worked. I'd show everyone that I would walk again.

Not only that, I would jump again. After all, I was Dolly Shepherd, the aeronaut.

But in the meantime, I wouldn't make Aunt Mariam any more worried than she already was.

"Did you say you have letters from Mother and David?" I asked her. "Would you read them to me?"

I listened to Aunt Mariam's soothing voice and lay back on my pillows. I needed to rest – before I got busy with recovering!

CHAPTER 13

The Whisper on the Wind

Just eight weeks later I was back. Who would have guessed? Dr Allan's treatments had worked wonderfully, along with the exercises he had created for me. Every day I'd pulled myself up by a rope fixed between the walls in my room, and I'd shuffled along the floor till my shuffles turned into confident steps.

And now I was marching. Marching towards Captain Gaudron and the balloon – with a brass band by my side!

"What is this?" I said, laughing.

"It's in honour of your comeback, Dolly!" the captain told me. He held an arm out so that he could lead me to my trapeze.

I took a deep breath as I stepped into the canvas sling and wrapped my fingers around the familiar wooden bar.

"Nervous?" Captain Gaudron asked me gently.

"Not at all," I replied.

But my tummy felt fluttery. Did I have the strength for this? To take my mind off any nerves, I chattered away while Captain Gaudron did his safety checks.

"I keep meaning to ask ..." I said. "After my accident, did you manage to find someone to jump the following Saturday? Or did you have to cancel the show?"

I expected Captain Gaudron to say that he jumped himself – or perhaps one of the men who assisted on the aeronaut display team.

But then the captain frowned.

"Didn't you know, Dolly?" he said with a surprised tone to his voice. "Your mother took your place!"

"My mother?" I repeated.

But there was no time to say any more. The balloon was lifting, swooping me up towards the clouds, and I was laughing. Laughing in sheer delight at flying again. Laughing as I pictured my darling mother sailing through the sky, breathless with the thrill of it.

And then I imagined the girls and women in the future who would do the same – or more. Maybe there would come a day when women would sit in actual flying machines and be transported for miles, from country to country!

Maybe girls like me would become pilots – not
just passengers – one day.

*

What a glorious return that was to my life in the air! And there were many more ... I lost count, but I think I completed about one hundred jumps in all.

Then came the day when everything changed. I was performing back where I'd started – at dear old Ally Pally. The weather was fine, the crowds were friendly, the solo balloon rose easily. I marvelled as I always did at the feeling of being totally free, all alone in the sky. It was as wonderful as it had ever been. And then I heard the whisper ... A whisper that seemed to arrive on a wisp of wind.

"*Don't come up here again,*" it said.

I froze, holding my breath. What was that?

"*Don't come up here again,*" I heard the whisper say softly but clearly.

I gazed around at the empty blue sky and the beautiful view. As I swayed I felt suddenly calm. I decided to accept the message and its meaning, however strange and unexpected it was.

"All right," I said aloud, and then pulled my cord.

My parachute puffed for one last time as I dropped and drifted towards the earth.

It was over. But I knew that my head – and my heart – would forever drift in the clouds …

CHAPTER 14
What Dolly Did Next

Dolly may have given up being an aeronaut, but her adventures were far from over. Just as Captain Gaudron predicted, manned flight developed very quickly, but so did events that led to the First World War. Dolly joined the Women's Emergency Corps, learning how to drive a truck. Soon after, she was in France, proving herself to be a fearless driver in enemy territory and a great mechanic.

After the war, Dolly married and had a daughter, Molly. But Dolly didn't settle down – first of all she became a children's social worker.

Then, as soon as the Second World War began, she enrolled as a fire marshal in the Blitz and found herself in charge of many community bomb shelters. She truly was an unstoppable force.

At the age of 88 Dolly was confined to a wheelchair. One day she went to watch the world-famous Red Devils parachute squad in action. She was delighted as they leapt in formation from jets flying above and floated down to earth. Dolly's daughter took her to meet the team afterwards so they could compare notes! The Red Devils realised what Dolly had done and invited her to fly with them. A short time later she found herself sitting in the co-pilot's seat of a jet, watching as the young parachutists leapt into the air below.

One of those parachutists was Jackie Smith, who was the first woman to join a military display team. Dolly watched her drift downwards towards the earth.

Many decades stretched between the two women. But they had one thing in common.

They were aeronauts.

Female daredevils.

Women who saw the whole of the sky.

Girls with their heads in the clouds ...

Dolly Shepherd lived to the age of 94 and got to see man walk on the moon. Her daughter, Molly, continued the family tradition as a parachutist. Molly celebrated one of her birthdays with a parachute jump – she was 83! Dolly, her mother and her daughter were truly three generations of brave and brilliant women.

Author's Note

Many years ago I moved from Scotland to London. Life in the big city was great fun, but it was busy and bustling and I did miss the wide open spaces of my home country.

Then one day I discovered a very special place in north London – Alexandra Palace, or Ally Pally, and the huge parklands around it. The palace sits high on a hill and the views from up there are just amazing! You can see all across London and spot famous buildings like St Paul's Cathedral, the London Eye, the Shard and the Olympic Park.

I decided that I really, really wanted to live close to Ally Pally, and once my husband Tom and I moved to our little flat, we'd go for a walk in the park nearly every day. Then I signed up for a history tour of the palace and that was it – I was hooked on the place!

Ally Pally has had such an interesting past. Lots of the entertainments I've mentioned in the book really took place there, but there are also sadder stories. For example, the palace was used as an internment camp where local Germans were held prisoner during the First World War. When I visit the park now, I can't help but think of the people who once walked along the same paths, from Victorians laughing and having wonderful days out, to the German-born men who had to talk to their wives and children through metal fencing in the grounds while the building was a temporary prison.

But the one person from Ally Pally's past who really caught my attention was Dolly Shepherd.

She was a very young woman when she started out as an aeronaut but went on to be so brave and independent. This wasn't easy in the days before women had the vote. I read everything I could find about her and was pleased to stumble on a rare copy of Dolly's autobiography (*When The 'Chute Went Up*). I already admired her, but reading this book I really got a sense of how cheerful and positive she was, as well as being an expert on aeronautics and flight.

And just as this book was going to press, I stumbled on yet another fascinating fact about Dolly: her daring double-descent with Louie-May made it into the famous *Guinness Book of World Records* as the First Mid-Air Rescue!

I'm still not completely sure where in the park the balloon flights took place, but I'll keep trying to find out. Meanwhile I go for my walks around Ally Pally and look up into the sky, imagining Dolly drifting happily up there ...

Our books are tested
for children and young people by
children and young people.

Thanks to everyone who consulted on
a manuscript for their time and effort in
helping us to make our books better
for our readers.